This
Little Tiger
book
belongs to:

- -

- -

- -

For Granny Black Hair and Granny White Hair
~ M P~T

For my stoic and wonderful nan, Thelma Gibson
~ K J M

LITTLE TIGER PRESS LTD,
an imprint of the Little Tiger Group
1 Coda Studios, 189 Munster Road, London SW6 6AW
www.littletiger.co.uk

First published in Great Britain 2018
This edition published 2019

Text by Maudie Powell-Tuck
Text copyright © Little Tiger Press Ltd 2018
Illustrations copyright © Karl James Mountford 2018
Karl James Mountford has asserted his right to be identified as the
illustrator of this work under the Copyright, Designs and Patents Act, 1988

A CIP catalogue record for this book is available from the British Library

Printed in China
LTP/1800/2656/0219

2 4 6 8 10 9 7 5 3 1

the SPACE TRAIN

Maudie Powell-Tuck

Karl James Mountford

LITTLE TIGER
LONDON

JAKOB'S LOG
01::04::2084
FORTUNA SPACE
STATION

Inventory 096:

1 Boy (me)

1 Granny

1 Robot chicken
(Derek)

1 ToolBot (grumpy)

22 Abandoned airlocks

10 Deserted decks

54 Hangars
(12 unexplored)

1 Alien living in the
trash compactor

0 New friends

1 Mysterious thing
found (further
investigation needed)

Jakob lived light years from Earth,
in a space station on the edge of a galaxy.
He had a granny, who would never sit still,
and a robot chicken called Derek.

Jakob also had a secret. Hidden away
in Hangar 19, he had found . . .

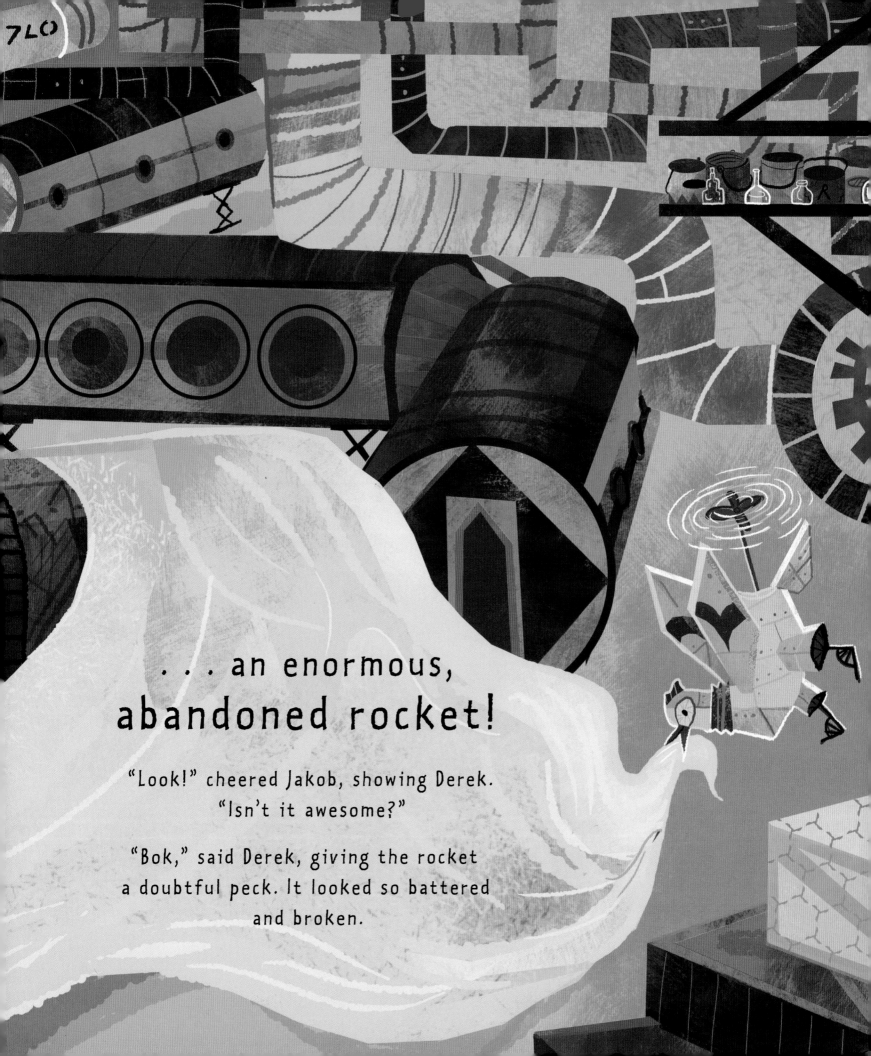

. . . an enormous, abandoned rocket!

"Look!" cheered Jakob, showing Derek. "Isn't it awesome?"

"Bok," said Derek, giving the rocket a doubtful peck. It looked so battered and broken.

But when Granny saw the machine,
she jigged on the spot.

"That's no rusty rocket, it's the SPACE TRAIN!" she cried, so loudly that Derek laid a screw in surprise.

"The Space Train?" asked Jakob, wrinkling his nose. "Bok?" clucked Derek. Both were utterly baffled.

"When I was little," said Granny,
pulling out her holoprojector,
"the Space Train criss-crossed the
universe on tracks of stardust,
visiting station after station—"

"How many stations?" interrupted
Jakob, who liked facts and figures.

"Two thousand, seven hundred
and forty-seven," Granny replied.
"You could spend a whole year on the
train and not see them all."

"Wow!" cried Jakob. "Was the Space Train fast?"

"Faster than the fastest spaceship.
So fast it made stars look like
streaks in the sky."

They creaked open a
carriage door and climbed inside
the grand, dusty dining car.
"Who rode the train?" Jakob asked.

"All sorts,"
Granny replied.
"Star explorers, comet
chasers and time travellers.
There were artists and scientists
too — and lots and lots of children."

Children, thought Jakob.
They could be my friends. "Granny,"
he said aloud. "We have to fix
this train!"

Then Derek laid nuts and bolts and anything else they might need . . .

while Jakob fetched Granny's ToolBot.

"I'm not coming," grumbled ToolBot. "I want to watch TV."
"Yes. You. Are," said Jakob, dragging him away.

Soon, everybody was ready.
"Let's begin," nodded Granny.
"ToolBot, pass me a wrench."

They worked all week, riveting,
welding, and fixing.

Jakob heaved lost wheels back into place, while Derek hammered loose valves. Granny whistled as she repaired the train's thrusters, and ToolBot sat around doing nothing.

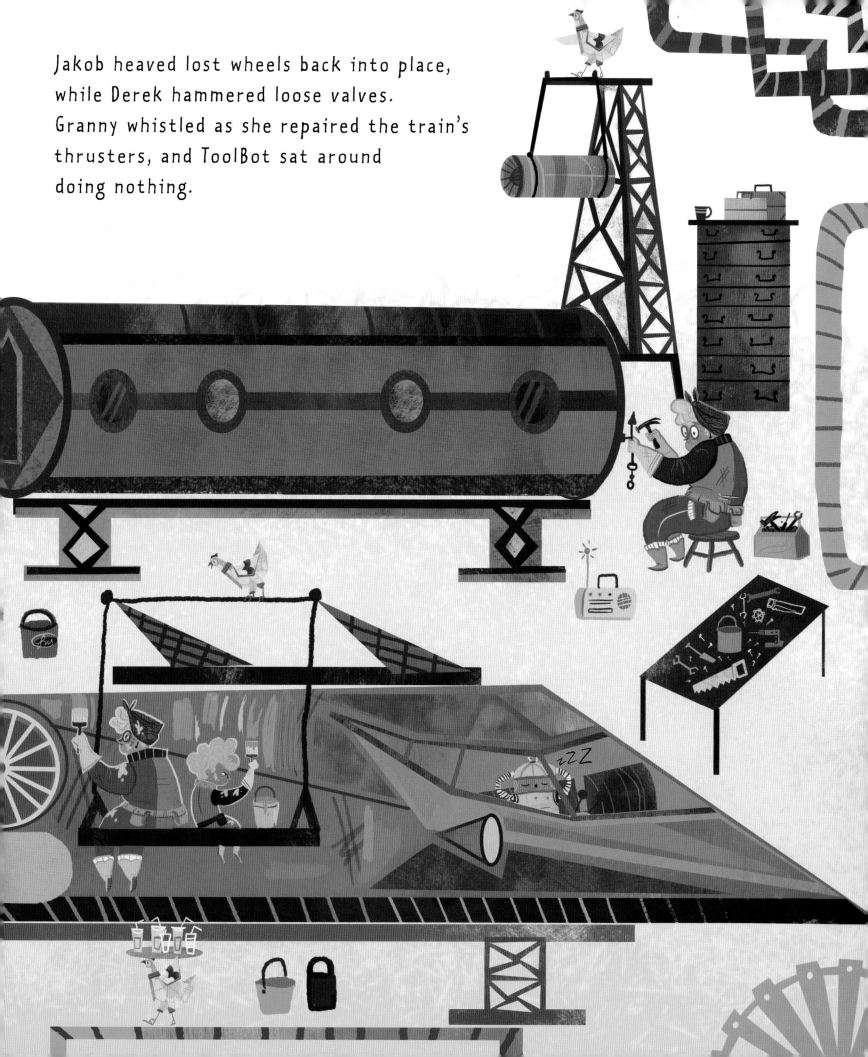

"Nearly done!" grinned Jakob as they
blast-cleaned the combustion chamber.
"Bok!" coughed Derek tiredly.

Finally, the train was ready.
"It's finished!" cheered Jakob, spinning Derek around.
"Can I watch TV now?" asked ToolBot.
"Bed," said Granny, firmly. "We'll launch the train in the morning."

That night, as a special treat, they slept out on the observation deck.

"Did you know that the Space Train can carry 200 passengers?" Jakob whispered to Derek, as Granny snored in her sleep pod.

JAKOB'S LOG
08::04::2084
FORTUNA SPACE
STATION

Top 3 people I want to meet on the Space Train:

1. A dinkybop (smallest creature in the universe!) from Planet Wooloo.

2. A star whale from the Flaming Moons of Kai.

3. Other boys and girls just like me.

P.S. I'm so excited!

The next morning, they all piled
into the train's cockpit.

"3...2...1...LIFT OFF!"

cried Jakob, pulling the launch lever.
The lights blinked on. The thrusters hissed.

"Chug-a-chug-a," huffed the train,

"chug-a-CLANK...

BANG!!

"Silly, stupid train!" shouted Jakob.
"We did all that work for nothing!"

"SQUAWK!" wailed Derek.
Even ToolBot was a little disappointed.

Granny gave them all a no-nonsense look.
"Everything can be fixed," she said firmly.
"Now don't just stand there like bottles of milk.
Find the problem and try again."

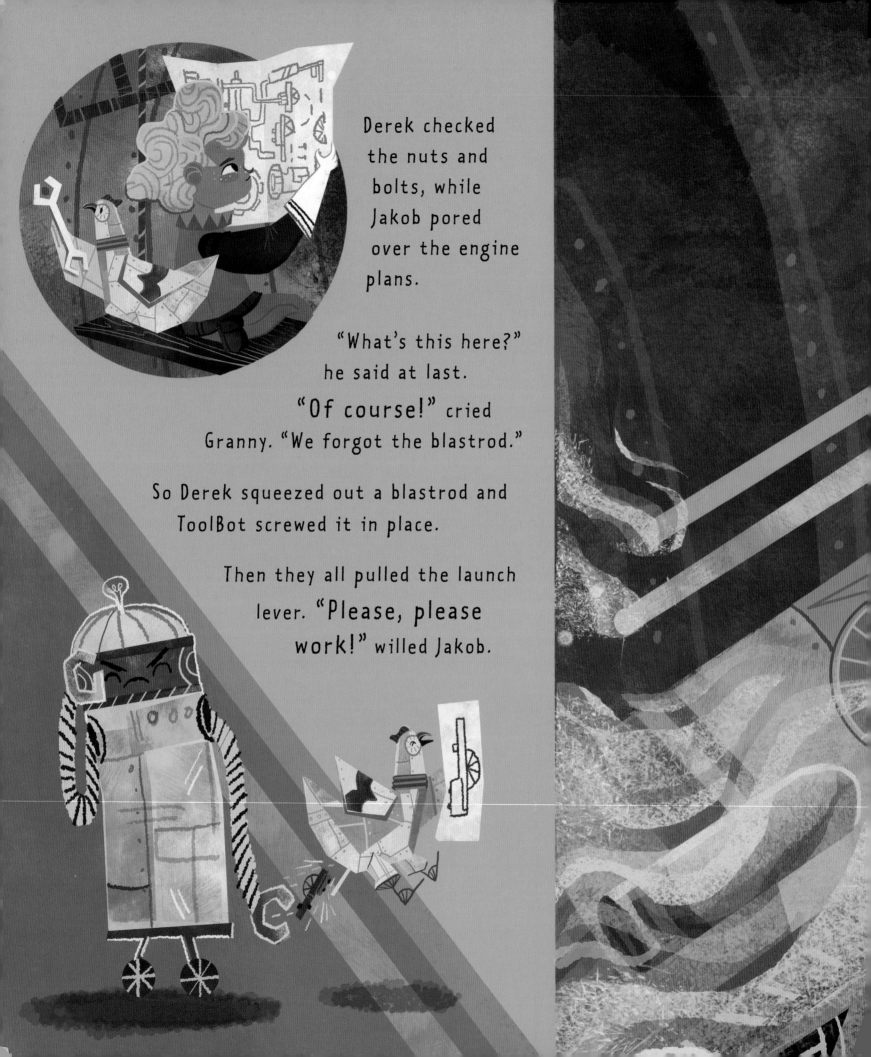

Derek checked the nuts and bolts, while Jakob pored over the engine plans.

"What's this here?" he said at last.

"Of course!" cried Granny. "We forgot the blastrod."

So Derek squeezed out a blastrod and ToolBot screwed it in place.

Then they all pulled the launch lever. "Please, please work!" willed Jakob.

The train jerked forward, the wheels began
to whirr and, hissing loudly, the Space Train
lifted up into the air!

"We did it!" cackled Granny, high-fiving Jakob.
"Fire up the rockets! Full steam ahead!"
And with a twist of the throttle . . .

. . . the train blasted off across space!
"Yippee!" whooped Granny. "Let's find new worlds . . ."
". . . and meet new friends!" cried Jakob.
And the Space Train sped off so fast,
the stars looked like streaks in the sky.

JAKOB'S LOG
02::03::2085
THE SPACE TRAIN

Inventory 118:

1 Boy (me)

1 Granny

1 Robot chicken (Derek)

1 ToolBot (less grumpy)

3 Galaxies, 39 planets visited

18 Comets chased

5 Star whales met

120 Passengers

120 New friends (yes!)

1,000,000,000,000 new adventures to have!

I met a dinkybop!

My new friends on the Moon of Elm

More extraordinary adventures from Karl James Mountford and Little Tiger Press!

For information regarding any of the above titles
or for our catalogue, please contact us:
Little Tiger Press Ltd, 1 Coda Studios, 189 Munster Road,
London SW6 6AW

• Tel: 020 7385 6333
• E-mail: contact@littletiger.co.uk
• www.littletiger.co.uk